Samuel French Acting Edition

Bobbie Clearly

by Alex Lubischer

FOR PRODUCTION ENQUIRIES

UNITED STATES AND CANADA
Info@SamuelFrench.com
1-866-598-8449

UNITED KINGDOM AND EUROPE
Plays@SamuelFrench.co.uk
020-7255-4302

Each title is subject to availability from Samuel French, depending upon country of performance. Please be aware that *BOBBIE CLEARLY* may not be licensed by Samuel French in your territory. Professional and amateur producers should contact the nearest Samuel French office or licensing partner to verify availability.

MUSIC USE NOTE

Licensees are solely responsible for obtaining formal written permission from copyright owners to use copyrighted music in the performance of this play and are strongly cautioned to do so. If no such permission is obtained by the licensee, then the licensee must use only original music that the licensee owns and controls. Licensees are solely responsible and liable for all music clearances and shall indemnify the copyright owners of the play(s) and their licensing agent, Samuel French, against any costs, expenses, losses and liabilities arising from the use of music by licensees. Please contact the appropriate music licensing authority in your territory for the rights to any incidental music.

IMPORTANT BILLING AND CREDIT REQUIREMENTS

If you have obtained performance rights to this title, please refer to your licensing agreement for important billing and credit requirements.

BOBBIE CLEARLY received its New York premiere produced by Roundabout Theatre Company (Todd Haimes, Artistic Director; Julia C. Levy, Executive Director; Sydney Beers, General Manager; Steve Dow, Chief Administration Officer) as part of the Roundabout Underground at the Harold and Miriam Steinberg Center for Theatre on April 3, 2018. The production was directed and choreographed by Will Davis, with dramaturgy by Jill Rafson, set design by Arnulfo Maldonado, costume design by Ásta Bennie Hostetter, lighting design by Jen Schriever, original music and sound design by Palmer Hefferan, and fight choreography by Lisa Kopitsky. The Stage Manager was Samantha Watson. The cast was as follows:

DARLA LONDON	Constance Shulman
DEREK NELSON	JD Taylor
MEGAN CURRIE	Talene Monahon
MEGHAN GOTSCHELL	Sasha Diamond
MITCH BACKES	Brian Quijada
PETE PFEIFER	Gabriel Brown
JANE WELCH	Crystal Finn
RUSS SCOTT	Marcus Ho
STANLEY WELCH	Christopher Innvar
BOBBIE CLEARLY	Ethan Dubin
EDDIE WELCH	Tyler Lea

BOBBIE CLEARLY received its premiere production at Steep Theatre Company (Peter Moore, Artistic Director; Kate Piatt-Eckert, Executive Director; Julia Siple, Managing Director) in Chicago, Illinois on September 29, 2016. The production was directed by Josh Sobel, with dramaturgy by Rebecca Adelsheim, set design by Eleanor Kahn, costume design by Brittany Dee Bodley, lighting design by Jeff Glass, sound design by Thomas Dixon, choreography by Jenna Schoppe, prop design by Jamie Karas, puppet design by Adam McAleavey, and fight choreography by R&D Choreography (Victor Bayona and Richard Gilbert). The Stage Manager was Lauren Lassus. The cast was as follows:

DARLA LONDON	Melissa Riemer
DEREK NELSON	Nick Horst
MEGAN CURRIE	Paloma Nozicka
MEGHAN GOTSCHELL	McKenzie Chinn
MITCH BACKES	Roy Gonzalez
PETE PFEIFER	Joel Reitsma
JANE WELCH	Erika Napoletano
RUSS SCOTT	Miguel Nunez
STANLEY WELCH	Tom Jansson
BOBBIE CLEARLY	Carson Schroeder
EDDIE WELCH	David Fisch

CHARACTERS

	2006 Age in Act I	2014 Age in Act II	2014 | 2017 Age in Act III
DARLA LONDON (w)	53	61	61 | 64
DEREK NELSON (m)	22	30	30 | 33
MEGAN CURRIE (w)	19	27	27 | 30
MEGHAN GOTSCHELL (w)	19	27	27 | 30
MITCH BACKES (m)	16	24	24 | 27
PETE PFEIFER (m)	16	24	24 | 27
RUSS SCOTT (m)	35	43	43 | 46
JANE WELCH (w)	39	47	47 | 50
STANLEY WELCH (m)	44	52	52 | 55
BOBBIE CLEARLY (m)	-	24	24 | -
EDDIE WELCH (m)	-	24	24 | 27

SETTING

Milton, Nebraska.
A small town of less than a thousand.
Technically, not even a town: a village.

AUTHOR'S NOTES

The play spans eleven years, but the age of each actor should roughly match the age of his or her character in Act Two.

The Welches and Bobbie are white. The rest of the casting is color-conscious and should be representative of both a small midwestern town and America.

If there are eleven white people on stage, something is wrong.

FONTS, PUNCTUATION, AND OTHER MARKINGS

Bold text denotes written letters that are read out loud.

(?)   A question disguised as a statement.

Example: The statement, "I think I'm going to the beach later.(?)" is a way of asking your crush to come with you, without having to pose it as a question.

*   Used in pairs. The character doesn't even stop to wait for the person speaking in between his or her lines.

Example:

DICK. I want a kitten*

JANE. Me too.

DICK. *and a puppy and a goldfish.

(**DICK** *doesn't stop speaking for one moment and runs over **JANE**'s line.*)

STYLE

This play is composed of interviews, recordings, and public presentations.

The audience is a group of interviewers and sometimes they are spectators at a public event.

The characters are always aware of the audience and speak to the audience.

They know they are being documented.

There are no private moments.

SET

An

acre

of

corn

hangs

above

a

bare

stage,

tassels down,

as

though

the

sky

is

the

earth.

ACT ONE

2006

*(**DARLA** enters in her police uniform.)*

DARLA. Now to tell you about Bobbie, I have to tell you about this other boy: Eddie.

I taught both of them in CCD.

It's an after school class for second graders at the public school so they can get their first communion.

I like to volunteer when I'm off duty.

I'm a volunteer-a-holic, my late husband George said.

Eddie Welch was this sweet kid. Very devout.

Knew: all of the answers. But <u>small</u>.

And Bobbie was always very <u>big</u> for their age group.

One of our breaks, Bobbie follows Eddie inside the boys' bathroom.

Pushes Eddie down. Won't let him out when he tries to get past him.

Eddie says, "Come on. We're going to be late to Officer Darla's class."

– They called me Officer, not "Mrs", from seeing me around town. I'm the only cop <u>in</u> Milton, Nebraska – it's a small town, 'bout eight hundred, so "Officer" is what they're used to –

Bobbie says, "You're right, we <u>are</u> going to be late to Officer Darla's class, unless you can think of a number that I'm thinking of between one and ten."

*(**DEREK** enters, apart from **DARLA**, in nursing scrubs.)*

DEREK. Bobbie was my little brother.

No! Sorry! Awkward! That's –

He wasn't my real –

I did this outreach thing two years ago as a sophomore in college where your title's "Big Brother." And Bobbie was my at-risk Lil Brah.

That summer(?) – oh-four *('04)* – Bobbie was iiiiiin Eigth Grade, yeah – We roadtripped to the College World Series. Huskers versus the Buckeyes.

Huskers kicked ass. It was awesome.

I was driving him back to Milton and he was like, Derek, can we go to the church?

Church? I'm like, I guess. What's up?

DARLA. So. Eddie guesses a number.

Say, five.

But it's the wrong number, Bobbie says.

So he slaps Eddie across the face.

And Bobbie tells him to guess another number.

Eddie says Nine.

But it's wrong, Bobbie says.

And so he slaps Eddie again.

But Eddie's not backing down because Eddie is one of those kids who thinks there actually <u>IS</u> a right number, and if he could just...

So he keeps guessing.

And he keeps guessing wrong.

And he keeps guessing wrong.

And he keeps guessing wrong

And finally he's guessed every number between One and Ten

And Eddie says, "It has to be one of those!"

To which Bobbie replies, "It's a <u>mixed</u> number."

DEREK. We go inside the church. They keep the doors unlocked! Who knew?

It's almost dark. Like only candles lit...

Bobbie starts playing piano, and I had no clue before.
It sounded like Coldplay but he told me it was, I don't
know, Bach? Something fancy and classical.
It was beautiful, dog.
I can still hear it.
That was his talent.

DARLA. And so Eddie starts guessing Mixed Numbers.
Five and one third.
Eight and three quarters.
One and one eighth.
And Bobbie keeps hitting him, until the side of Eddie's
face is a giant purple bruise and he can barely open his
mouth.
And Bobbie screams, finally, and I hear this down the
hall,
"Why won't you admit that you don't know?!"

DEREK. *(Excited.)* Am I your first interview?
No?
S'okay.
Is this documentary really for PBS?
Wouldn't it be crazy if this got nominated for an Oscar
like Lord of the Rings?

DARLA. That was seven years before the cornfield.

DEREK. What fucks me up is that was a week before the
cornfield.

DARLA. We honestly don't know why he did it.

DEREK. What did I not do?

DARLA. Which is what you'd really like to know. I'm aware.
So would I.

DARLA & DEREK. After the cornfield, Bobbie stopped
speaking to anyone.

DARLA. But he did hand the judge a tiny letter of apology.
I have it memorized. Would you like to hear it?
**"Hi. My name is Bobbie. I am really sad inside about everything.
My thoughts and prayers are with Casey and her family. I really
want people to know the real Bobbie someday. Sincerely."**

(**DARLA** *exits.*)

DEREK. Look, people can say what they want and I'm gonna piss some people off here but I don't care, it's been two years and I –
Bobbie's sort of like bizarro me.(?) Like all of my qualities: Reverse them.
Everybody wants to include me.
Just because like – I look a certain way, and so people like me, you know?
I got this internship so fucking easy. Cuz like I wanna be a male nurse, and there's not a lot of male nurses so this internship was like mine like that.
(*Snaps fingers.*) And I like pussy, so thank god, right, that's like this whole other – and my life would be this whole other – if like. And I'm American, you know.(?) People always say, "You look so all-American."

(*…*)

I wish Bobbie <u>was</u> my <u>real brother.</u>
I would like a brother who I could give a chance to.

(**DEREK** *exits.*)

(**MEGAN** *and* **MEGHAN** *enter. One wears a lifeguard uniform; the other wears a fast-food uniform.*)

MEGAN. Casey was more than my friend. She was like my little sister.
We would… Ha. Casey and I were obsessed with Christina Aguilera(?)*

MEGHAN. -Ha! Yeah.

MEGAN. *And we heard this rumor that the reason she looked so amazing was she did a thousand sit-ups a day and so <u>we</u> tried doing a thousand sit-ups a day.
Together. High-fiving.
Anyway it did not work and Casey and I got so sick.

(Laughter. Then sadness. Then:)

But now <u>we're</u> super close! *(Meaning Meghan.)* so, there is a silver lining.

MEGHAN. Yeah totally.

MEGAN. *(Off something the interviewer says.)* Oh so it's without the H, just regular Megan.
C. U. R. R. I. E. Like curry, like Indian curry.
Except it's pronounced CURE-ee. Like Madame Curie.
I'm nineteen.

MEGHAN. Do you want my name? M. E. G. <u>H</u>. A. N.

MEGAN. We're best friends AND we're both Megan. Isn't that weird? Isn't that bizarre? I think it's weird. We're so different.

MEGHAN. I wonder if our names have anything to do with us being friends, like, psychology. Like do you know?

MEGAN. Yeah. I've thought about that.

MEGHAN. I've thought about it A LOT. I think it might. You know? I think it might.

MEGAN. That summer? Detasseling?
The three of us were inseparable.

MEGHAN. Which is weird, because we were also Casey's – (?) She's technically under us.

MEGAN. Her bosses she means. That wasn't a dead joke.

(They're both mortified. **MEGHAN** *maybe mouths "No.")*

In detasseling there's always two managers.(?)

MEGHAN. Well there's like one head manager and onnnne, VICE manager?

MEGAN. But we like to think of it as co-managers.

MEGHAN. We were co-managers yeah. Megan and I.

MEGAN. Casey was a great detasseler! Bobbie was awful.

MEGHAN. His work wasn't –

MEGAN. Fuck Him.

   (**MITCH** *enters, apart from* **MEGAN** *and* **MEGHAN**, *and slurps his already-opened Sunkist. There's a second can, unopened. He starts shaking it.*)

MEGHAN. Yeah uhm. Well the big one was –

MEGAN. We didn't know what he was going to do. How could we have known?

MEGHAN. It's not like we could fire everyone.(?) Mitch and Pete were the best detasselers.

   (**PETE** *enters.* **MITCH** *hands him the shook-up Sunkist.*)

MITCH. Pete and me were best buds with Casey's brother Eddie.

PETE. Yeah we –

   (**PETE**'s *Sunkist explodes!*)

Shoot!

MITCH. Shit!

PETE. No!

MITCH. Stupid!

PETE. Shut up! (*Laughs.*) / You're stupid!

   (**PETE** *punches* **MITCH** *in the arm.* **MITCH** *laughs.*)

MITCH. (*To us.*) Can you get that in there?!

PETE. (*To us.*) NO! Yeah! Okay!

MITCH. I don't mind you recording us. Obviously. I signed the form.

PETE. Me too.

MITCH. We would always stay over at Eddie's house.

PETE. Play Mario Kart.

MITCH. Battle Mode!

PETE. (*Laughing.*) We would go to bed FURIOUS.

MITCH. He goes to a private school in Omaha now. He transferred after the cornfield.

PETE. We don't hang out that often anymore.

MITCH. But he calls me.

PETE. He calls you?

MITCH. Yeah he started calling me about a year ago.

PETE. *(Disbelief.)* I don't talk on the phone with anybody. I feel like guys don't talk on the phone. *(Unbelievable.)* Do you have <u>conversations</u>?

MITCH. *(Nods, coolly.)*

PETE. Whoa...

That summer, before it happened, I saw Eddie all the time, though. We'd ride four-wheelers. Go swimming. Even detasseling / could be fun.

MITCH. Should we tell 'em about...

PETE & MITCH. *(Are we going to say it together? Sssssssshhhhh – You're saying it? We're going there? – Enanigans?!)* Shhhhhhhhhhhenanigans?!

MITCH. Yeaaa/aaaah

PETE. Yeaa/ahh

MITCH. Yeaa/aah

PETE. There were some shenanigans.

MITCH. We'd take those tassels we were plucking off the corn and throw em at each other.

PETE. "Tassel fights."

MITCH. "Tassel Fights!"

PETE. We'd be running up and down the rows –

MITCH. <u>Hopping</u> to see over them and <u>chucking</u> tassels down at the person in the rows closest to you!

PETE. Well one day me and Mitch and Eddie Welch were in the middle of a tassel fight <u>melee</u>!

MITCH. Bobbie jumped in there and he threw one, too. Hit Eddie right in the face

PETE. On accident.

MITCH. Only Eddie didn't think it was funny,

PETE. Because of the whole second grade thing, / and also

MITCH. Plus Bobbie was just off! Nobody –

PETE. To play games like that, you have to –

MITCH. Bobbie didn't get what we were doing.

PETE. What <u>anybody</u> was doing.

MITCH. What real kids are like. So Eddie told Bobbie to fuck off.

PETE. Eddie was taller than Bobbie then. A lot bigger.

MITCH. And Bobbie <u>wouldn't</u>, I guess, fuck off. He kept throwing tassels.

PETE. And things escalated.

MITCH. Needless to say we got in a fight.

PETE. A FIGHT fight.

MITCH. All four of us.

PETE. Three of us versus Bobbie.

MITCH. Bobbie <u>started</u> the fight.

PETE. Well.

MITCH. But obviously, if that had anything to do with what happened… Bobbie overreacted and it's not our fault.

PETE.	MEGAN.
But.	But who are you going to believe?

> (**PETE** *and* **MITCH** *exit.*)

MEGHAN. That afternoon we said, "Bobbie –

MEGAN. He was a mess. Like a puddle on the gravel. Disgusting snot.
He couldn't stop sobbing. I was worried he couldn't breathe.

MEGHAN. Me too. I was.

MEGAN. It was like, have you seen PLATOON? There's that scene where they're like executing Vietnamese kids, like little Vietnam kids and old women and their families.(?)

MEGHAN. *(Disappointed.)* Oh, I've never seen it.

MEGAN. And it was like he was some Vietnam child and I was Kevin Dillon.

MEGHAN. Yeah, I couldn't do it. And I've <u>fired</u> people before.

MEGAN. And I've <u>watched</u> people get fired before? and <u>I</u> couldn't do it.

MEGHAN. But we let him stay on the team,

MEGAN. and so he knew what field –

MEGHAN. And two days later –

MEGAN. Sunday.

MEGHAN. It was July Fourteenth.

MEGAN. ...

MEGHAN. That was our mistake. Compassion, I think.

    (**MEGAN** *exits.*)

I should go. Sorry. I feel so bad for Megan.
She was the head manager.

    (**MEGHAN** *exits.*)

    (**DARLA** *enters.*)

DARLA. I quit teaching CCD the next year and started giving talks, in uniform, to junior high students and high schoolers, too. Mainly about drinking. I'd speak to teenagers who would go out "roadtripping" on weekends. That's when they get a hold of a 30-pack of beer and down the whole thing cruising back country roads. And I'd talk about being nice to other kids and I even helped arrange a food drive with the last nun alive here and we raised a bunch of food for the soup kitchen in Omaha. Anyway. I'm not trying to say I'm Mother Teresa, but there you go. Well so eventually that's how I got in contact with Bobbie the second time around.

    (**DARLA** *exits.*)

    (**RUSS** *enters with a guitar and cool facial hair.*)

> *(JANE enters with him, carrying a clipboard with a pen attached.)*

RUSS. Milton's got – We're calling it "Milton's Got Talent," after America's Got Talent. *(Plays faux-reality-show-host.)* "Because I think this place really does have a lot of talent, Jane."

JANE. *(Does the same.)* "I think so too, Russ. Lots of talented folks here." We have two students picked out to host it. Yeah, I have a little background in performance. And I interned at 10/11 News like eighteen years ago but you get a feeling for onscreen performance. I interned for the weather girl. And Russ was a theater major in college.

RUSS. Fun Times.

JANE. So anyway.

RUSS. We wanted to bring this to Milton for Jane's daughter. I feel like there IS so much talent here, and if we could bring folks together –

JANE. It's been two years. We're ready to – yeah. And it's for a scholarship. I think it's the right thing. And there's gonna be kool-aid, and macaroons and scotcheroos and... Snickers! People are bringing candy bars.

RUSS. It's free.

JANE. Yep. Free. They let us just have the church basement[1] for free, it's such a good – It's gonna be so fun. We're taking sign-ups right now. You should look at the clipboard. We're going to sing a duet we've been practicing. We're both huge fans of Jewel, and we've been getting a lot of inspiration from "Pieces of You."

RUSS. Oh. I think that is – Oh. I love that.

---

1. The location of the talent show should be linked to the space where *Bobbie Clearly* is being performed. For the Roundabout Underground production, "church basement" matched the underground performance space. If the play is being performed in a more traditional proscenium, Jane may say "community center."

JANE. But that's gonna be part of the show. That we're organizing. This music gives me a lot of strength and this community gives me a lot of strength. And Russ gives me A LOT of strength. Friends do that, you know. And – and it's been hard. But you know you can either look into your own pit of despair I think and that is a well that goes and down and down and there is no bottom – so why bother, you know – or you can turn out and face the world and try to do things for others and really build a legacy.(?)

> (**STANLEY** *enters, apart from* **JANE** *and* **RUSS**, *in camouflage and hunter orange.*)

STANLEY. Jane asked me to do this Talent Show thing. I said, "Why?" She said, "Don't you want to be part of the community?" I said, "I have to do this to be that?" She said, "I think it might be nice for you." I said, "You're not a psychiatrist." She said, "Then see a psychiatrist then." I said, "No." She said, "Then help me do this one thing, please." I said, "Alright, alright, but Friday I'm deer hunting." Deer season's only two weeks long. I just knew this would be my last shot at a buck. Tomorrow we'll be helping Jane all with the set up. Me and my son – OUR son. Jane's son. Jane's and my son. Our kid. We'll be helping her and Russ with the set up. And that's fine. And then Sunday is the Talent Show. Hunting is not Jane's thing. But she likes jerky. Me, I love it out here. This had always been my thing with – Uhm.

JANE. This whole talent show is for.

JANE & STANLEY. Casey.

JANE. I think, "Would Casey be wanting me to go into this hole?"*

STANLEY. Casey loved hunting.*

JANE. *"No."

STANLEY. *It was our father-daughter time thing.

JANE. It's for her memory. For her.

STANLEY. She screamed out, "YAHOO!" when she got her first buck.*

JANE. She was always such a performer.*

STANLEY. *Literally "Yahoooooo!"*

JANE. *She was on the dance squad.

STANLEY. *We called him Beginner's Luck. The head's still mounted on the den wall.

JANE. She was Sally Bowles in Rent –
    er, no Cabaret. Sorry. I always get those two mixed up. Both so racy.
    She was Gwendolen in The Importance of Being Earnest!
    That one's my favorite. I showed Russ the video.

RUSS. I thought: WOW. You know?

JANE. She was going to win an Oscar someday.*

STANLEY. She was a natural born hunter.*

JANE. *I know it.

STANLEY. *(I was so proud that.) I didn't even make her help me with the cleaning part.

JANE. Stanley's healing his own w – he has / his – uhm.

STANLEY. Any time with my son – OUR son – That's helpful for me.

JANE. But that's okay.

STANLEY. It doesn't <u>have to</u> be hunting.
    Sitting watching movies with him is helpful.
    Seeing his wrestling meet is helpful.
    Driving him and his girlfriend to their first date at Pizza Hut is helpful.
    I don't like being alone so much.

JANE. Stanley <u>likes</u> being alone.
    But different people are different. And that's okay.*

STANLEY. Jane was always the talker.*

JANE. *I think Stanley just wants to put everything away in a box,*

STANLEY. *Always wanting to go go go to basketball games*

JANE. *which you can't do. I can't.*

STANLEY. *and to be the Dance Mom and I'm older is part of it.*

JANE. *He's never been much of a people person, Stanley.

STANLEY. *How I got so lucky I don't know.

JANE. Actually I'm really very lucky. It takes a toll. And he's been – I love him. He's the father of my children. But Stanley doesn't sing so it was nice to find just like a good friend who really liked to sing.

RUSS. Yeah. Uhm. Yeah. Totally.

JANE. I've never told him this, *(Meaning **RUSS**.)* but I was SO WORRIED, you know, that Stanley would be threatened by Russ or, you know, jealous, because you know men, and just like – He wasn't at all. He wasn't at all threatened. Even if I had wanted him to be he wasn't. Which I didn't.

RUSS. *(Smiling.)* Yeah. He's –

JANE. *(To **RUSS**.)* Hey, you should play the guitar chords you learned. And the picking? *(To us.)* He's gotten so good. I get chills.

RUSS. Okay.

JANE. Play. Just listening I get chills.

> *(**RUSS** plays something in the style of "You Were Meant For Me" by Jewel[1] on the guitar. **JANE** hums occasionally.)*

---

1. A license to produce *Bobbie Clearly* does not include a performance license for "You Were Meant For Me" by Jewel. The publisher and author suggest that the licensee contact ASCAP or BMI to ascertain the music publisher and contact such music publisher to license or acquire permission for performance of the song. If a license or permission is unattainable for "You Were Meant For Me," the licensee may not use the song in *Bobbie Clearly* but may create an original composition in a similar style or use a similar song in the public domain. For further information, please see Music Use Note on page 3.

STANLEY. But I like father-son time. With my son. OUR son. Jane's and my son. Part of it is I know that he's safe with me. I know nothing bad would happen to him in front of me. And if it did... But uh.

JANE. I like to be still and listen.

STANLEY. I thought my hunting days must be over. Because I thought – it was Casey's thing with Dad. HA. But here we are, me and him, and it's nice. He misses his big sister. He was in the cornfield with her, you know, when it happened. He won't talk to anybody about it. Nobody.

JANE. I know Casey's going to be in that room with us.

STANLEY. Eddie's up in the tree stand.

(**STANLEY** *exits alone.*)

(**JANE** *and* **RUSS** *exit together.*)

(**DARLA** *enters.*)

DARLA. Bobbie would always be sitting there in the very back at my talks, not engaging. I didn't like him much, tell you the truth.

Then three years ago, when he was thirteen, he smashed ten windows in city hall. All along the front. I gave testimony at the vandalism hearing. You can read it in the transcripts. He got not much: community service, probation. I gave him the private number at the station. And my cell. People need someone to call and some people don't have any people. For whatever reason.

Well time goes by and it's...two summers ago. I get a call. It's, oh...eleven or so in the morning. Bright and sunny. Hot. A few clouds in the sky, maybe two and the rest blue. You can hear the corn growing. That kind of day. July Fourteenth.

(**DARLA** *exits.*)

(**PETE** *and* **MITCH** *enter. They are alone on stage at the talent show. They are dressed in suits that are too big for them. One of them is a tan suit.*)

PETE. WOOOO!!! LET'S GIVE IT UP FOR GUS WAGNER!

MITCH. GUS WAGNER! WOOOOO!!!

PETE. That was some great Muppet Acting.

MITCH. Uh, Ventriloquism Pete.

PETE. VenTRILoquism. Gotcha. You know I'd never seen a real live dummy before?

MITCH. Really? That's surprising.

PETE. Why's that?

MITCH. You ever looked in a mirror?

(*He points at* **PETE** *with two index fingers. Hold for groans?*)

PETE. Ah man, that's – (...) But you know what my favorite food is?

MITCH. What's that Pete?

PETE. Gotta be Flaming Hot Cheetohs. They're so hot they had to take em out of the vending machines cuz all the little fat kids were eating too many. "Hot! Hot! Hot!" (*Mimes shoving more into his mouth.*) You gotta shove more into your mouth to stop the spicy!

MITCH. That's what she said.

DEREK, FROM THE BACK OF THE AUDITORIUM. This is a family show!

PETE. Uh, Flaming Hot Cheetohs are so hot, they make the Huskers' offensive line look not-so-hot.

MITCH. They're so hot they're hotter than your Mom.

PETE. This guy.

(*Punches* **MITCH** *playfully in the arm.*)

MITCH. <u>This</u> guy.

(*Punches* **PETE** *harder in the arm.*)

> (**PETE** *tries to rub his arm without anybody noticing he's rubbing his arm.*)

MITCH. Well we want to say thank you to Mrs. Welch and Russ for putting this on –

PETE. and giving us our first hosting gig –

MITCH. It's been a real honor –

PETE. and you guys have been a great crowd –

MITCH. And to <u>Mr.</u> Welch too, who bowls with my dad. I know the queso dip is your specialty and you bought all the pop. So –

PETE. yeah, thanks Mr. Welch. And this is for –

MITCH. Casey was the first girl I ever kissed so I'm glad we can honor her this way, you know? Personally.

> *(…)*

PETE. We have one more act for you to close out the night! They're former Milton Senior High co-captains of the dance team, they're all the way back from college. Let's give a big round of applause for *(Checks in with* **MITCH.***)* Meghan Gotschell.

MITCH & PETE. And

MITCH. Megan Currie!

MITCH & PETE. Lots of applause!

> *(They applaud and yell "Wooooo!!!!! Woohoo!!!" as they exit the stage.)*

> *(**MEGHAN** and **MEGAN** enter in matching sparkly getups.)*

> *(They didn't spend a ton of money on this, but it's not overly gaudy or tacky.)*

> *(They probably spent an evening making these outfits and they both look nice.)*

> *(They wave to the crowd.)*

MEGHAN. Hi everyone.

MEGAN. Hiiiiiii.

> *(They check in with each other.)*

MEGHAN. So.

MEGAN. So we were on the dance squad, like they said. We were co-captains.

MEGHAN. Well really, Megan was the captain but I was sort of –

MEGAN. She did all the organizing and we were basically co-captains.

MEGHAN. Basically.

MEGAN. And I could never do a cartwheel.
Wow, I'm so nervous. Feel my pulse.

(**MEGHAN** *does.*)

MEGHAN. She's real nervous.

DEREK, FROM THE BACK OF THE AUDITORIUM. *(Well-meaning.)* Don't Be!

MEGAN. Thank you! So we had a lot of debate about what we should perform tonight and why. But we decided… Well we were thinking of course there were a lot of slow and meaningful dances we could do.

MEGHAN. And they actually might be easier.

MEGAN. Maybe. Yeah. But. Then we were like, "Who wants to be sad?" And this isn't about being sad.

MEGHAN. I mean if people are sad that's okay though.

MEGAN. But. Yeah. But. This is for Casey Welch.

MEGHAN. And her parents, and her little brother, Eddie, who is staying home today but I know he's here in spirit, and – you know – for Jane. Especially Jane. Who was such a cool Mom. I've always looked up to you.

MEGAN. And this was one of Casey's favorite artists and one of her favorite songs.

MEGHAN. Some of you might remember it.

MEGAN. And we have a special guest.

MEGHAN. And this special guest has stage fright cuz boys are dumb but just wait.

MEGAN. Just wait.

MEGHAN. Just you wait.

MEGAN. You know there's this great quote. It's from –
(Checks in with **MEGHAN**. *Grins.)*
Okay I'll just say it!

> *(She takes a tiny square of paper out of
> her bra and unfolds it and reads from it.
> **MEGHAN** will silently mouth parts she has
> memorized.)*

"From the oldest of times, people danced for a number
of reasons. They danced in prayer…or so that their
crops would be plentiful…or so their hunt would be
good. And they danced to stay physically fit…and show
their community spirit. And they danced to celebrate.
And that is the dancing we're talking about. Aren't we
told in Psalm 149, "Praise ye the Lord. Sing unto the
Lord a new song. Let them praise His name in the
dance"? Ecclesiastes assures us that there is a time for
every purpose under heaven. A time to laugh…and a
time to weep. A time to mourn…and there is a time to
dance. See, this is our time to dance!"

> *(She folds up her paper and puts it back in
> her bra.)*

MEGHAN. Kevin Bacon said that.

> *(**MEGHAN** exits.)*

MEGAN. *(Looking offstage to **MEGHAN**, smiling nervously.)*
I've always wanted to say…

> *(Deep breath.)*

"HIT IT!"

> *(An infections/terrible song starts playing.)*

(For instance, let's say the song is in the style of "Breathe" by Michelle Branch[1].)

(The music is really loud.)

(**MEGAN** *dances.*)

(She's out of sync with the song at first. She's a little self-conscious. If there are words, she mouths the words silently and you can tell she's trying to remember the moves. We should be a little afraid for her. This is a dance tribute at a memorial talent show: a lot could go wrong.)

(It's okay if this is mind-blowingly awesome for the audience.)

(It's okay if this is uncomfortable for the audience.)

(It's okay if it's both.)

(The beat picks up.)

(**MEGHAN** *enters.*)

(**MEGAN** *gets new confidence. A lot of their choreography is perfectly synced. They alternate between dancing facing the crowd and dancing facing each other. Lots of eye contact and checking in with each other.)*

(The first chorus is impressive.)

---

1. A license to produce *Bobbie Clearly* does not include a performance license for "Breathe" by Michelle Branch. The publisher and author suggest that the licensee contact ASCAP or BMI to ascertain the music publisher and contact such music publisher to license or acquire permission for performance of the song. If a license or permission is unattainable for "Breathe" the licensee may not use the song in *Bobbie Clearly* but may create an original composition in a similar style or use a similar song in the public domain. For further information, please see Music Use Note on page 3.

(Verse two: They incorporate ribbon dancing.)

*(***MEGHAN*** does really awesome cartwheels! ***MEGAN*** cheers!)*

(Second chorus: A costume change. They incorporate silly string.)

(Bridge after second chorus:)

*(***DEREK NELSON*** comes onstage from the wings in a rock star costume and does a dance solo.[1])*

MEGAN & MEGHAN. DEREK NELSON!

*(***PETE*** and ***MITCH*** come onstage and join the dance. They're not pros, but they've been given a specific set of limited choreography and they nail it.)*

*(Final chorus: ***DEREK*** and ***MEGHAN*** and ***MEGAN*** and ***PETE*** and ***MITCH*** all dance together. Things can get pretty sloppy now, but it's fun and really fucking cathartic.)*

(The song ends.)

(They're breathless.)

(If there is applause, they bow.)

*(If there is no applause, they just exit together, smiling, and maybe ***DEREK*** bows anyway out of habit, self-consciously.)*

*(***DARLA*** enters. She is not at the talent show.)*

DARLA. I answer the phone. I hear his voice on the other end. Takes me a moment. But I hear his voice and he's saying... He tells me what he's done. He calls me from Casey's cell phone. He'd memorized my number.

---

1. Or plays a sax solo, if it fits the song.

I drove out there. I don't have any jurisdiction outside of town but I drove out there. I called 911 on the way. I called him back on my cell. I said, "Wait there. Do not leave."

The corn looked the same. Like nothing had happened any different. Just standing there in barely a breeze. And I knew he was somewhere inside, and so was Casey Welch. And I wondered if there were any others in the field.

There was one bird on the telephone wire and no cars on the gravel roads. All quiet.

I went in. I started yelling, "Bobbie! Bobbie!" Calling his name. Answer me, I'd yell. Tell me where you are.

You can't see two feet in front of you in that corn. Not at my height. If you hop you can see a little ways ahead. But if someone's sitting on the ground or perched, you'd run into 'em before you'd see them.

A gun fires in the middle of the field. To my left and up ahead. I move toward the sound. Unholster my seven-shooter.

(Pause.)

He's sitting right beside her and the rifle's pointing in the air. Straight up.

I take it by the stock – he let's me – and I put it on the ground behind me. The ground is wet. It rained the night before. First rain in a month.

I don't remember the last thing he said. Something unimportant. Not teary. Like he was sitting at a dinner table asking pass the peas.

I thought – I really did – for the first time in many years that maybe there are some who do not deserve life. And I debated whether I was gonna say this next part or not but I wanted to shoot him.

But I didn't.

I marched him very slowly out of the field.

DARLA. He didn't say nothing the whole time and I didn't ask nothing. We had to leave the girl there. I felt bad about that. I bent a cornstalk down against the dirt when we reached the end-rows, so I could see it coming back like a bookmark and know which row to walk down and find her.

It wasn't till I got him in the car that I could look back, and saw corn rustling away in the distance. A survivor. Who could have been long gone by now, but he's been hiding and waiting, not wanting to leave his sister. I wanted to go to him, but I had to stay with Bobbie.

It took the troopers and the ambulances so long. We were out in the middle of nowhere.

I've been thinking about Bobbie lately. With Christmas coming up. And Advent. I think about what he's thinking about. I think about what he's spending his time doing in that facility, where no one can visit except for family once a month and of course they've moved out of state by now. I think about who's thinking about him. And every week in church there's another candle lit. And it got to be the pink one last week and they did the Town Nativity on the practice football field and that meant only one more week left till Christmas and I thought –

I tried writing him a letter. It's unsent. It's a Christmas Card.

Shit, I'll just read it.

(*She takes out a letter.*)

"Dear Bobbie..."

(*Silence.*)

I can't read it out loud.

You get the gist. I think I should send it.(?) Probably. It's only a Christmas Card. I send them to people I don't even like. Plus, it's already stamped. They're expensive. I'll send him just this one.

(**BOBBIE** *enters. He wears nondescript clothes.*)

(He looks at **DARLA**, *who looks at him.)*

(This can take a lot of time.)

*(***DARLA*** goes to him and hands him a Christmas card.)*

*(***BOBBIE*** reads it.)*

(He smiles.)

(He folds it carefully.)

(He honors it.)

*(***DARLA*** goes to leave.)*

(She stops.)

(She turns.)

(She goes to **BOBBIE**.*)*

(She gives him seven more Christmas Cards, one at a time, each in festive, colorful envelopes.)

(There is ritual in the giving.)

*(***BOBBIE*** honors every one.)*

*(***BOBBIE*** hands **DARLA** a stark white envelope.)*

*(***DARLA*** opens it.)*

(She starts to read, silently.)

(She looks at **BOBBIE**.*)*

(She looks at us.)

*(***BOBBIE*** gives her permission, silently.)*

*(***DARLA*** reads the letter out loud while **BOBBIE** fastidiously dons a button-down shirt. Something he could wear to church or a job interview.)*

DARLA. "Dear Darla,

I have saved every one of your Christmas Cards.

When I was sixteen, when I got the first one I thought, "Treasure this. You'll never get another one." But I did. You kept sending them. Every Christmas I look forward to getting another one of your cards, and hearing about what is going on in your life and what is going on in Milton.

This year, though, there is something that I am looking forward to even more than one of your letters: I am being released in March, the day after my twenty-fourth birthday. It's a great birthday present, haha.

I am moving back to Milton. I will be moving in with my cousin, and his girlfriend, and their dogs.

I have changed so, so much Darla. I truly believe now that everything happens for a reason. I'm better now, and this has given me the chance to start my life over again, and bring light into the world, and really make good on what happened in the past.

I know that you'll hardly even recognize me in person, and that you'll see what a good, good change I've made for the better. Everybody will be so surprised.

Love,

Bobbie"

End of Act One

Intermission

ACT TWO

2014

(There's a piano onstage, apart from **EDDIE** *dressed for his job.)*

EDDIE. *(Faux-chipper sales pitch.)* "Welcome to Apple, my name's Eddie! My sister was murdered in a cornfield ten years ago, would you be interested in checking out our new MacBook Air?!"

A month ago I got the Creative promotion.

You're a Genius or a Creative and now I'm a Creative.

That feels good. Knowing, you know?

No job is perfect but I get weekends off and that's great because I'm trying to build my board game business.

What else can I tell you that's interesting?

I'm an atheist.

And I'm gay.

That was a shock for my parents.

Both of them.

And Russ, but Russ takes most things in stride. He's cool with like whatever.

I talk to my parents about everything: even gay stuff.

We have no secrets.

I think my sister being murdered, uhm, made most things in life easier for me and made my relationship with my parents – sort of insured it? if that makes sense. And I don't care if it doesn't actually. My ex-boyfriend – I won't even say his name – doesn't think I should be so blunt about my dead sister, or how that's helped me,

or hurt me. Well he thinks because he can't imagine it.
But it's actually quite easy <u>to imagine</u>.
Imagine your sister dying.

> *(Waits for us to have to…)*

> *(Then, upbeat.)*

EDDIE. <u>And</u> the remarkable thing is that you'd get over it!
You would.
Ninety-nine percent of people <u>would get over it</u>! I don't
mean that it wouldn't haunt them or they wouldn't
wake up like once of year from nightmares about
running through cornfields, but from a functional like,
"does this iPad work" standpoint, "does this board game
have achievable objective" standpoint – on that kind of
basis ninety-nine percent of people would get over it.
That's what you <u>want</u> me to talk about, isn't it?
Not my job.
Or how I went to DePaul.
Or living in Boystown.
Or my Tap Class.
Not my life now.
You want to talk about ten years ago.
<u>That</u> part of me.
Specifically.
Alright.

> *(**BOBBIE** enters.)*

> *(He sits at the piano.)*

> *(He plays Franz Schubert's "Impromptu No 2
> in E-Flat Major, D 899" or something in the
> style of Coldplay's "The Scientist."[1])*

---

[1] A license to produce *Bobbie Clearly* does not include a performance
license for "The Scientist" by Coldplay. The publisher and author suggest
that the licensee contact ASCAP or BMI to ascertain the music publisher
and contact such music publisher to license or acquire permission for
performance of the song. If a license or permission is unattainable for
"The Scientist" then the licensee may not use the song in *Bobbie Clearly*.
For further information, please see Music Use Note on page 3.

(He's amazing.)

(He underscores **EDDIE**, *pianissimo.)*

*(***EDDIE*** *has told this story a lot, but never to cameras.)*

I was out there showing my sister how to detassel. To help her. I was fourteen, she was sixteen. I'd always been short but then in puberty I really hit a growth spurt. Lucky, huh? I had done detasseling the summer before, but Casey was always pretty delicate. Kind of a nerd? And I was always uhm...relatively tough.

(Chuckles.) She was so funny. She was Gwendolen in The Importance of Being Earnest? She was so funny in that.

(He relives a good memory for two seconds.)

But delicate.

uh That summer she wanted to make some money to buy a...oh god what was it... To have a CD player installed in her car. It was her first summer job and she was shorter than the other kids and like I said, delicate, and she was behind everyone else in terms of productivity. Everybody <u>else</u> had finished two sections and Casey was still on her first. And at the end of the work day Saturday, Meg(h)an said that Casey was behind schedule and that even though they were friends, Casey had to have that section walked by Monday or else Meg(h)an would give Casey's sections to somebody else. Somebody better. And then she wouldn't be able to buy that CD player.

Bobbie hadn't finished his either. So it was just them.

They were the bad detasselers.

So then on Sunday, July Fourteenth, even though we were <u>supposed</u> to have that day off, I went out there to help her walk her sections after church. We were going to bang em out. Just the two of us. Alone.

Except it wasn't just the two of us.

EDDIE. Obviously.

There were three of us out there.

And I was in the tall corn walking in front of my sister and...

> (**DARLA** *enters in her police uniform, holding a letter.*)

Sorry.

This is my first time talking about it. Out in the open.

To strangers.

> (*She reads the letter.*)

DARLA. **Dear Darla,**

EDDIE. I get a little angry.

DARLA. **Please let me know what you think of this version.**

EDDIE. Because it's like, I didn't choose it.

It's like, you take the Defining –

DARLA. **You might be asking,**

EDDIE. "Who is Eddie Welch?'"

DARLA. **"Who is Robert Clearly?"**

EDDIE. Define him.

DARLA. **Well.**

EDDIE. If I had to pitch myself to God.

DARLA. **If I thought hard about it.**

EDDIE. And say, "Hey, this is what you're getting. Buy me. Buy this product."

DARLA. **And really racked my brains.**

EDDIE. And I had to list the parts of my being, like my fucking like essence,

DARLA. **Let me tell you.**

EDDIE. It would obviously be the parts I had no control over.

Male.

DARLA. **Hard worker.**

EDDIE. Gay.

DARLA. Team player.

EDDIE. Born on a farm.

DARLA. Handy. And

EDDIE. My sister was murdered in front of me.

DARLA. I Hate Flies!

EDDIE. Except what's – What makes me so – What makes me cry actually –

DARLA. I Really Hate Flies.

EDDIE. because I can't – Because I cry when I get angry which is really hard for like confrontations with upper management, and breakups.

DARLA. I really really really hate them.

EDDIE. What fucking destroys me is that I didn't get to Choose any of those:

DARLA. More than the average person.
Actually, probably about the same amount.

EDDIE. Male.

DARLA. Yours

EDDIE. Gay.

DARLA. Truly

EDDIE. Farmboy.

DARLA. Robert

EDDIE. My sister was murdered in front of me.

DARLA. Clearly.

EDDIE. And the fourth one like... That's something that was inflicted on me by another person, but a person lower than a person, lower than...

DARLA. P.S. I have included Darla London's phone number.
She is my character reference.

(**DARLA** *exits.*)

(**BOBBIE** *exits.*)

EDDIE. Bobbie hasn't tried to contact me ever. Even since
he got out. But if he did, I mean, I would write him
back. I would <u>have</u> a conversation with him. I would
honestly share all the ways in which I've grown, and
maybe the ways in which I'm still pretty uhm w –
I would forgive him.
Not because he deserves it.
But because to <u>not</u> forgive somebody,
to carry that,
everyday,
I'm done with all that.
I would ask him, "Why?"
Because...not knowing?
If I could understand, then...
Because it's this thing that changed you permanently
and you're not given any clear...
So yeah, sure, sometimes I have to get in my Saturn
and drive because in a big city your car is the only place
where you can scream and not be heard, but I think
that's most people.(?)

    (**EDDIE** *exits.*)

    (*Enter* **PETE** *and* **MITCH** *drinking beers. They're
    outside at night, dressed for late fall.*)

PETE. Mitch drives a truck now.

MITCH. Peterbilt. They're the best kind.
It's a big eighteen-wheeler.
And Pete owns a gas station!

PETE. Two. Count 'em: Two.

MITCH. I haul fuel for ethanol companies.

PETE. Most gas in your cars now has ethanol in it. They get
it from –

MITCH. Corncobs.

PETE. Big Money.

MITCH. Big Money.

PETE. B-bb-b-b-b

MITCH. B-b-b-b-/ b-bb

PETE. BIiiii/IIIG

MITCH. BiiiiG

PETE. b-b-bBIIIIIIIG

MITCH & PETE. Biiiiiig Money.

> (**MEGAN** *and* **MEGHAN** *enter apart from* **PETE** *and* **MITCH**.)

> (*They are doing some task together in preparation for the upcoming talent show. Making costumes, hanging streamers – it could be anything.*)

MEGAN. Soooo

MITCH. Shit.

PETE. Shoot.

MEGAN. We wrote a Book.

MEGHAN. Well Megan wrote a book and basically – I helped.

MEGAN. I mean yes, but like basically we're co-Authors. Co-EDITORS.

MEGHAN. Co-Editors. / Yeah. Right. Exactly.

PETE. I've stayed put in Milton. Settled down here.

MITCH. And I'm down in Florida.

MEGAN. It's called *Pieces of Casey: A Collection of Interviews*.

MEGHAN. We got the inspiration from Jewel.

PETE. But we've stayed close.

MITCH. Really close.

PETE. Best Man-close.

MEGAN. We're practically like sisters.

PETE. (*Beams.*) Mitch was the best man in my wedding.

MEGAN. Meghan was my bridesmaid.

MEGHAN. And Megan was MY Maid of Honor.

MEGAN. Meghan WOULD have been my maid of honor except for my Real sister who I kind of had to put in there.
Oh my god, Harry's *(Meghan's husband.)* the sweetest guy.

MEGHAN. And Megan's married to Doug Hanson

MEGAN. *(To the interviewers.)* It's great that you're back.

MITCH. I always make the journey back.

MEGAN. *(To the interviewers.)* I feel like nowadays people <u>watch</u> documentaries.(?)

MEGHAN. *(To the interviewers.)* Will the sequel be streamed?

PETE. Me and Mitch have hosted <u>all</u> <u>eight</u> <u>talent</u> <u>shows</u>.

MITCH. Back to back to / back to

PETE. Back to

MITCH & PETE. BAAAAAAA // AAAAAAAACK

MEGAN. This year we're doing the talent show again.

PETE, MITCH, MEGHAN & MEGAN. Together.

MEGHAN. Gonna be a blast from the past.

PETE. Like Mario Bros. Like Mario and Luigi. Just a couple'a buds. Savin the world, savin the princess, warpin the zones –

MITCH. Yeah –

PETE. Hoppin the koopas –

MITCH. The first one was such a big –

PETE. Takin the pipes –

MITCH. Yeah. Hit. They decided to make an institution out of it.

PETE. The Casey G. Welch Foundation

MITCH. It's a big ass 501(c)(3).

MEGAN. We're going to read an excerpt from my – Our book.

MEGHAN. A spoken word piece.

MEGAN. A choreopoem.

MEGAN. I always get so nervous

MEGHAN. So we've been working on her stage fright.

MEGAN. And we've been working on her stage PRESENCE. I mean it's just been stressful in general here, since Bobbie moved back.

MEGHAN. It's been about seven months.

MITCH. Yeah, we gotta work on our comedy routine, bud! And we gotta talk about the lineup and plan out our jokes and –

PETE. Hey, I gotta pee. I'm gonna run into the station quick. But, Yes to all that.

> (**PETE** *exits.*)

> (**MITCH** *takes his wallet and keys out of his pockets, sets them down, and drinks under the light of the gas station marquee.*)

> (**DARLA** *enters with a letter.*)

> (**BOBBIE** *is clipping his fingernails.*)

DARLA. Dear Darla,

I have my first real job! A permanent job with thirty-nine hours a week! I'm going to live here!

I work at the Flytrap Factory now! On the assembly line! I cited you as a reference and I'm pretty sure that's what cinched it. I love you I love you I love you I am so filled with LOVE for you, Darla!

I've already learned the trick to being a <u>great</u> team member!

Do not go too fast: your coworkers will be mad at you. But do not go too slow, either: then your <u>bosses</u> will be mad at you.

<u>Go exactly the right amount.</u>

Everybody has their role, the <u>correct</u> role, and everybody must work efficiently and at the same pace or else. Well. You know.

I'm going to have friends and coworkers! and I bet in a year or two I'll grumble about the job to them, my coworkers, but really, I'll be grateful. I'll say, "In today's economy what with the so and so," and we'll get hot wings and chow down at TGI Fridays.

I feel like that's going to happen.

>   (BOBBIE *finishes clipping his fingernails. Looks at them. Smiles.*)

DARLA. I feel so normal, Darla. So normal and good.

>   (BOBBIE *exits.*)

>   (DARLA *exits.*)

>   (DEREK *enters apart from* MEGAN *and* MEGHAN.)

MEGAN. He's affected my life in huge ways.

DEREK. Oh Totally.

MEGAN. Like, I lock my door now.

DEREK. I've hung out with him.

MEGAN. I never locked my door before.

DEREK. I hang out with him all the time.

MEGAN. Doug bought a handgun.

DEREK. He's just a person, you know?

MEGAN. I don't let my daughter go the park by herself.

MEGHAN. And we never had to do that in the past.

DEREK. I found out he was going to my girlfriend's church. Cheyenne, that's my G.F. Our church isn't like the old one, the judge-y one, the Catholic one? It's newer. Cooler. Opener. More accepting. Some pop music is okay too! And we incorporate that into like, our worship. Not stuffy stuff like "There's A Wideness in God's Mercy." Although that IS true.

>   (DEREK *exits.*)

MEGHAN. The Catholic parish bazaar was a month ago. Right during harvest time.*

MEGAN. Bobbie showed up –

MEGHAN. *They put up a big tent behind the high school gym.

And I'm working the ring toss station, because I volunteer.

MEGAN. I got her this fuchsia t-shirt that says, "Stop me before I volunteer again!"

MEGHAN. And it's my FAVORITE t-shirt but it HASN'T stopped me.

MEGAN. *(Ominous.)* Bobbie showed up. To play ring toss.

MEGHAN. He was really bad. Clumsy.

MEGAN. *(Ominous.)* Yeah.

MEGHAN. But nothing out of the ordinary.

MEGAN. Wasn't he there, though, like…?

MEGHAN. *(…)*

MEGAN. So my thing is…

I had this TRAUMATIC experience with Bobbie at the supermarket.

I was picking –

MEGHAN. Actually I got a text from Harry. I'm gonna – Can I – ? I'll be right back.

*(**MEGHAN** exits.)*

MEGAN. I was picking up ingredients to make stuffed peppers: Doug's favorite. But so I'm in line at the checkout counter, and my two-year-old's in the grocery cart with his

*(**MEGHAN** reenters.)*

cute little chubby legs poking out and Allison's standing beside me asking politely for a candy bar, and all of a sudden Aly shuts up and her eyes get wide. And I knew. I knew he was behind me. I wondered what he was buying. Turns out it was all meat: Two pounds of ribeye. *(Ominously.)* Yeah. And then he whispered, "You have a beautiful – ."

MEGHAN. I mean, it wasn't that dramatic, was it?

MEGAN. What do you mean?

MEGHAN. *(A look.)* Essentially – and your truth, your experience, that's super important to me.

MEGAN. Thank you.

MEGHAN. He.

   He was behind you in line. Which happens at –

MEGAN. Sure.(?)

MEGHAN. It was uncomfortable.(?)

MEGAN. He stalked your ring toss.

MEGHAN. He was bad at ring toss and stubborn about
   being bad at ring toss but...

MEGAN. *(A look.)*

MEGHAN. He didn't do anything.

MEGAN. This isn't what we talked about.

MEGHAN. I'm sure it was scary.

   I'm not trying to –

   I don't think he meant to freak you out.

MEGAN. "How do you know"

MEGHAN. I looked back. At the. First one. And. I don't
   know. We're twenty-seven? now. *(Almost like she's
   asking for permission.)* I feel a little differently.(?)

MEGAN. Okay. Hmm. Okay.

   I'm sorry I just

   I don't understand. This is...

   I feel like we're getting a little heated. Which is –

   (Change Topic.) The important thing is the talent show.

MEGHAN. I don't feel comfortable with this.(?) anymore.
   (?) And.

   I wanted to say that for myself.

MEGAN. *(What do you mean by "This"?)* What?

MEGHAN. *(Gestures to* **MEGHAN**, *to the cameras, to us.)*
   THIS. This. All of this.

   (Pause.)

   (Eye contact.)

MEGAN. Okaaaaay, when did you decide – ?

MEGHAN. It's not about – *(You.)*
    It's –
    I'm not gonna do it anymore, Megan.
    It's a lie that for the last three years
    I've missed the talent show because that's the only time
    Harry's work will let him go on vacation.
    It's the middle of November:
    that would be cruel and unusual of his factory to do
    that.
    We go at that time because I want to miss it.
    I'm another person.
    I'm not nineteen.
    Why are we in this?

MEGAN. Oh my god.

MEGHAN. Look, one of the things I admired about you so
    much is like you are
    (To the interviewers.) – she is –
    In high school you could have been honestly the biggest
    bitch*

MEGAN. Meghan –

MEGHAN. *But BUT you weren't.
    (To the interviewers.) She wasn't.
    I wasn't very cool,
    Casey wasn't very cool –

MEGAN. I drive thirty miles away now, and buy all of my
    groceries from Wal-Mart.(?)

MEGHAN. Look it's legit that you took Casey under your
    wing.
    I didn't. You did.
    So I do understand if this whole thing is bigger – *(For
    you.)*

MEGAN. We wrote this book.

MEGHAN. <u>You</u> wrote this book, and I helped

MEGAN. Yeah, less and less and less / and –

MEGHAN. Because I'm embarrassed, Megan.
I don't want him to be so BIG in my life.
I don't want Casey to be such a big part of my life.
If Eddie, and Jane, and Stanley want to do this
(...)
They should.
But.
This isn't mine.(?)

MEGAN. What happened ten years ago was the worst thing
that ever happened to me.

MEGHAN. It didn't happen to you.

MEGAN. *(This next part is very hard to say.)* Do you even
like me?

MEGHAN. Megan, don't.

MEGAN. I'm sorry I don't have the right thing to say always.
I know people laugh at me.
I know people...
God you know, it would be so fucking nice to be taken
seriously for once.
You weren't the head manager.

> *(To the interviewers.)*

And neither were – *(You.)*
And you're not <u>from here!</u>
You're not from a small town.
We had a graduating class of twenty-one.
And Casey's was <u>supposed to have</u> nineteen.
And it's easy to talk about forgiveness and blah blah
blah and judge.
When you don't have to <u>see</u> that m –
<u>Person</u>. Everyday.

> *(Pause. **MEGHAN** decides to wrap this up, to
> the cameras.)*

MEGHAN. But I'm really looking forward to the talent show
this year.

MEGAN. Yeah. It's literally the only thing in town that's sacred anymore.

(**MEGAN** *and* **MEGHAN** *exit.*)

(**DEREK** *enters.*)

DEREK. So the next week I made it a point to go to church. Bobbie was there by the coffee bar. He looked really scared. Like a lost deer. Like childhood Bambi. It's Bobbie, me, and my girlfriend in a pew, and I'm in the middle – my daughter's on my lap – holding Bobbie's hand, squeezing Cheyenne's hand, because I'm so excited. So excited for Bobbie. Like, "Here is a chance for pure Christianity." End Quote. Like when you extract THC from a thing of marijuana and condense that shit into little Nilla Wafers? It's like that except WWJD points to the nTH degree! AND HE KEPT COMING BACK AND HE KEPT SITTING BY US! And the next week he started playing piano. And do you know he is the BEST pianist we've ever had? And eventually... I invited him to our house one day for brunch.

(**DEREK** *exits.*)

(**PETE** *reenters with two new beers.*)

MITCH. That was long.

PETE. Yeah. I thought I just had to pee but then I realized I had to poop too.

MITCH. Yeah. I know what that's like. Did you wash your hands?

PETE. No.

MITCH. Fucker.

(*They grin. They clink.* **MITCH** *takes a swig.*)

PETE. Every year I mark my calendar for the week that Mitch comes back

Big red sharpie. Mitch Mitch Mitch!

MITCH. Pete Pete Pete! Me too! About you!

Hey, we gotta get crackin on our comedy routine, bud! This has gotta be the best one yet!

PETE. Yeah. Yeah! I agree. Especially cuz Bobbie's signed up
  this year.

> *(S)*

> *(I)*

> *(L)*

> *(E)*

> *(N)*

> *(C)*

> *(E)*

> (**MITCH** *bursts out laughing.*)

> (**PETE** *laughs with him.* **PETE** *stops laughing.*)

> (**MITCH** *keeps laughing.*)

MITCH. I thought you were serious for like two seconds!

PETE. Hah.

MITCH. That's good. That's REALLY good. That would be
  something, wouldn't it? Like if you hadn't told me and
  I had literally driven one thousand miles to be here and
  then you like, dropped that on me the week of. In front
  of people.

PETE. yeah

MITCH. But it would make sense right, cuz you were nervous
  and...ha...that's funny.

> (**PETE** *smiles.*)

> (**MITCH** *smiles.*)

> (*They look at each other for a long time.*)

  Pete.

PETE. I should have told you. He did sign up.

MITCH. But you told him no, right?

PETE. It says anybody can apply. That's the whole point.(?) On the website. "Bring communities together, bring awareness to –" There's no bylaws or –

MITCH. Who else knows about this?

PETE. Uh Nobody –

MITCH. Okay –

PETE. You and me and uhm… *(Gestures to the audience.)* Mitch. He's SIGNED UP.

MITCH. Well, I didn't <u>know</u> about it. So. I didn't <u>approve</u>.

PETE. Yeah, but.

MITCH. Yeah but what? … *(Whispers.)* Pete can I talk to you in private about this?

PETE. It took him forever to get a job, you know? Last week somebody egged his cousin's car. In June they spray painted "GIRL KILLER" on the side of his house. And all he wants to do is / make amends –

MITCH. You don't know what he wants.

PETE. And he comes to ME and says, "Please let me be a part of this. I've been saving up my paychecks. I've saved up five hundred dollars – almost two weeks worth of wages – which I'm going to donate." And he put it on my counter. His hands were shaking. And I think… I don't know. Isn't that what – What Jesus – ?

MITCH. We Skype every week. Every Tuesday.

PETE. Okay but –

MITCH. When did he sign up?

PETE. A month ago.

MITCH. That's Five Tuesdays Man!

PETE. Because I knew you would –

MITCH. And then you tell me in front of… Now?! Like when you broke up with your girlfriend at that really popular Applebee's?!

PETE. Nobody's "breaking up with – "

MITCH. And you hoped because it was crowded on game day she wouldn't make a scene? Did you think I would go along with it? To look good?

PETE. No!

MITCH. You're saying it's okay. That ten years in a hippie dippie –

PETE. Prison?

MITCH. For crazy people. Not a real / prison

PETE. For juvenile's / who were children when

MITCH. Was adequate and now –

PETE. And you think it's not?

MITCH. At fourteen you know right from wrong! I lost my virginity at fourteen. I shoplifted at fourteen. I took my driving test for a school permit so I could drive into school from the country at fourteen. Those are adult decisions. He can't take it back. Cas – Eddie's sister is still dead. Jesus what do you think Eddie's gonna – ? Or Jane? Huh? What about Mr. Welch? What would They Do?

PETE. Bobbie lives here now. He's part of this –

MITCH. He SHOULDN'T be Living Here –

PETE. But he does, Mitch. And you don't. I see Bobbie every week in church. I see you once a year. I live here. He lives here. I work here. He works here. I see people walking through the streets, having babies, going to work, buying new cars, filling them up, I wave to them, I know all their names. And so does Bobbie. I know what's best for this town, better than you could. There's a reason why I'm Head Organizer –

MITCH. We're CO-organizers. And CO-hosts –

PETE. I mean I like to think of it that way but...

MITCH. But What?

PETE. When push comes to shove...

　　(...)

MITCH. Wow. WOW. I'm fuckin out.

(**MITCH** *walks over to his keys and wallet.* **PETE** *grabs them first.*)

PETE. I shouldn't have told you this way.

MITCH. Give me my keys.

PETE. I was nervous. I was wrong. It was dumb. But I can't take it back.

MITCH. Hey, you're the head organizer, Pete. I guess it's your show. I guess you can do what you want.

PETE. I don't want to have to do it without you.

MITCH. <u>You</u> could change your mind. Because it won't be me changing mine. *(…)* Give me my keys, man.

(**PETE** *does.* **MITCH** *walks away.*)

PETE. Don't you feel bad?

MITCH. Why would <u>we</u> feel bad about Anything?

(**MITCH** *exits.*)

(**PETE** *chugs the rest of his beer.*)

(**DEREK** *enters.*)

DEREK. Cheyenne was a little nervous about brunch. But I said, "Shy-shy, we do this? We do it ALL the way." After brunch Bobbie rode bikes with our daughter, and I think he's really great with kids, actually. Cheyenne showed him her hemp knitting and Bobbie told us he'd been practicing sewing and crafts. He was so so gracious for that little slice of normalcy. By then it was midday and we'd put Kendra down for her nap. And Bobbie whispered, "You have a beautiful family." "Do you want a beer?" I said. And Bobbie said he wasn't allowed to have substances. But I said, "Come on man. One will not hurt." And then he had a Coors! And do you know what?! Do you know what?! It was his FIRST TIME EVER DRINKING A BEER! Isn't that crazy?! Yeah. And <u>I</u> gave it to him!
And then we had a threesome.

(*Silence.*)

DEREK. You should have seen your face! *(Laughs.)* No we didn't have a threesome! What kind of a freak do you think I am?! Jesus! God. But we ARE friends.
This weekend we're going out just the two of us. Bro Night!

> *(***DEREK*** *exits.*)*

PETE. Don't put that in there. Leave all of this out, okay? Mitch will change his mind. There's plenty of time. We've got

PETE & JANE. Five days until the Talent Show.

JANE. I get a call.

> *(***PETE*** *exits.*)*

> *(***JANE*** *enters.*)*

Anonymously. It's an anonymous caller and he – I mean she... They Tell me.
I feel punched in the gut. I feel...
"Is this a practical joke?" I think.
How Could He? You know?
I went to six years of therapy just to begin to –
But maybe it's not in the universe yet and if I –
You won't believe this. I call Peter. I say, "Is this true?"
Peter asks who told me, so I tell him. He says, "Yes. It's true."
I say, "Well, Remove him obviously!" Right?
Peter says No.

> *(Laughs.)*

I say: "Okay."
So we call the board of directors. Ten men. I'm on it too but I'm not the president. I'm just one vote. Somehow.
I say to the president, "This has to be stopped."
They say, "We'll think about it."
"Think about it?!" I say. "It's Four Days Away."
I can't stop thinking about it. It's all I can –

Russ and I were going to sing a song from Cabaret because that was her –

> (**STANLEY** *enters apart from* **JANE**. *He wears camouflage and hunter orange. He has two knives and a bucket. He puts everything in its right place.*)

Of course Eddie would never be in the same Talent Show as Bobbie, and he was so excited. This was gonna be his first – .

So I hear back from the board. A full day passes during which, of course, I can't do anything. I'm paralyzed. And there is so much to get done, believe you me.

Somebody's leaked it to the news.

That he's enrolled.

STANLEY. First we'll string him up from the bough of this cedar. Head down, so the blood drains.

> (*The carcass can be real or invisible, but we see all of the motions of gutting and dressing.*)

JANE. And now we can't do anything about it, they say. How negative would that look? How "unchristian." They tell ME, it would look unchristian.

STANLEY. I use two knives: I use a fillet knife and I use a skinner knife with a skinner hook on it.

JANE. For the past ten years I have done nothing – NOTHING – but serve others.

STANLEY. People recommend you use the rubber gloves but I don't.

JANE. This has really made an impact you know, it has.

STANLEY. The goal is to remove everything out of the deer.

JANE. I go to these communities,

STANLEY. I do it here in the field,

JANE. people have lost somebody.

STANLEY. because he's heavy.

JANE. Sometimes it's ten people and there are ten families…
you know…it's a huge wound.

STANLEY. Find the bottom of the sternum. Make an
incision.

JANE. And we come together. People share their talents.

STANLEY. Put your fingers in there. Two. Ooo. He's sticky.
Put the knife between your fingers. Slide the blade up
the belly to between his hind legs. Mind the goodies.

> (**STANLEY** *does this carefully. It takes time.*)

JANE. Senator Buchner (*Pronounced* <u>Buekner</u>, *like Bueller.*)
wrote us a letter in 2012. To Jane and the Casey G.
Welch foundation. It's framed in my living room.

STANLEY. Two…finger…shuffle…

JANE. All I do is try to serve and be a good person. I don't
know what to do. Is this what God is asking? Is he
saying, "That's not enough, Jane. That's not enough.
All the work you've done, all the lives you've touched,
that's not enough. You have to Forgive Bobbie." – I
HAVE forgiven him – But that's not enough. "You have
to let him in your talent show. You have to invite him
to Thanksgiving and Christmas at your house and give
him presents and take a selfie with him." It's too much.
I can't. And I shouldn't be asked. But it feels like that's
what everyone's demanding.
Am I a bad person?

> (**JANE** *sobs.*)

> (**STANLEY** *finishes.*)

STANLEY. Poor Buck. He's all split out. Now we'll take out
the insides.

> (*He does this silently throughout the rest of
> the scene. It involves flaying hide and cutting
> bone and ablating organs and depositing
> them in the bucket.*)

JANE. The board says this looks so positive. It's really – ughck, I want to vomit – Looks Full Circle. But if we kick him out...we'll look like bad people. WE'LL. LOOK LIKE. BAD. PEOPLE. HILARIOUS! Wouldn't want THAT.

I think okay. Okay. Okay. What do I do?

> (**RUSS** *enters.*)

RUSS. What did I miss?

JANE. Nothing Russ. Hi. I'm telling them about...

RUSS. Are you doing okay?

JANE. I don't know.

RUSS. I love you.

JANE. Thanks.

RUSS. Despicable, huh? Him doing this.

JANE. Mmm-hmm.

RUSS. He's twisting the knife, you know? Just twisting the knife.

JANE. That's what – I think so too! And Stanley said, Stanley's just trying to be a son of a bitch. Stanley says – oh I hate him – (*A* **STANLEY** *impression.*) "Maybe he's trying to contribute. Maybe he wants to honor Casey's memory." Except Stanley really doesn't feel that way, obviously.

RUSS. Honey.

JANE. Sorry. I shouldn't say – I don't mean that. Stanley's a good man. He's the father of my children. He's the love of my life.

RUSS. Well.

JANE. Anyway, so I thought, (*To* **RUSS**.) Can I show them the letter?

RUSS. I don't know if that's a good idea.

JANE. (*To us.*) I'm gonna show you. Here. It's here on my phone.

> (*She takes out an iPhone. She clears her throat. Scrolls.*)

JANE. Let me find it. Okay.

> **"Dear Bobbie,**
>
> **It has come to my attention..."**

>> *(She stops reading.)*

I can't read it out loud.

>> *(She sobs. **RUSS** puts his hand on her shoulder. Tentatively.)*

STANLEY. And that's how you field dress a Whitetail Buck. I don't mind that Bobbie's performing. I think it's great!

JANE. It's three days away

STANLEY. That's what the talent show is all about, right? He's one of us now. Clearly. You know, I might go. Eddie's signed up. Yeah, Eddie's doing an act this year. Should be a fun time. See you there.

>> *(**STANLEY** exits.)*

>> *(**JANE** stops sobbing. She stiffens.)*

RUSS. What? *(...)* Honey?

JANE. *(Paralyzed.)* He's calling me.

RUSS. What?!

JANE. He's calling me. It's on silent. He's calling.

RUSS. Oh.

JANE. You answer it.

RUSS. What?

JANE. I won't – I can't answer it. I can't – RUSS!

>> *(**RUSS** takes the phone.)*

RUSS. UhmOkayHiHellOO?

>> *(He walks across the room, making eye contact with **JANE** and us periodically. He paces when he talks.)*

Robert! Hi! *(.)* This is Russ. *(.)* Russ, Jane's husband. *(.)* No I'm her husband. *(.)* Uh yep. Yep they did. *(.)* Nope that wasn't just a rumor. *(.)* No it's always good to check. It's okay. *(.)* Ssss *(Raspberries.)* Soooooo how are youuuu? *(.)* Great. Good.

JANE. Russ.

RUSS. oh i'm, You Know. Uhm. ...Isabe – Our daughter's seven now. So uhm. That's fun.

JANE. *(Whispers.)* Russel.

RUSS. I mean, pretty bad actually. Well. In the middle. Depending.

JANE. *(Whispers.)* What's he saying?

RUSS. Yeah, uhm, we're gearing up for the talent show. *(.)* Yeah I know! I saw that! *(.)* Oh you GOT the letter. That's great. Yes. Uhm. *(.)* Uhm *(Looks at* **JANE.***)* ... actually...she is...in the bathroom. *(.)* Uhh. Nope she won't be available then either. She uhm...can't talk. Very busy. *(.)* No but she WANTS to talk –

JANE. Tell him I don't want to talk to him.

RUSS. She doesn't want to talk to you. But. I would LOVE to talk to you. Have you given any thought to uhm resign – leav – stepping down from the talent – *(.)* Oh you haven't? *(.)* Uh-huh. *(.)* Uh-huh OkAAAY. *(.)* Uhm...well maybe Reconsider because...?

JANE. Russ. You had better get him to –

RUSS. Actually that's uhh...uh... Not okay. Uhm. We're both pretty angry.*(?)* Like the letter says. And uhm. We want you to step down. God dammit. It's important so – *(.)* No I understand that, but – *(A great idea!)* Hey maybe just record yourself! Send in a tape. Then – Would that be / good?!

JANE. *(Whispers.)* Give me that fucking phone.

RUSS. Bobbie, I don't think you can presume to know what Casey would want.

JANE. What did he say?

RUSS. Well we sure wish you would reconsider.

(**JANE** *grabs the phone from* **RUSS.***)*

JANE. This is Jane. Listen to me.

> *(.)*

He hung up.

> *(She dials his number. Puts the phone to her ear. Waits.)*

He's not picking up.

RUSS. Do you want to leave a voicemail?

> *(**JANE** ends the call.)*

> *(**JANE** leaves town.)*

> *(**RUSS** is alone.)*

> *(**RUSS** exits a different way.)*

> *(**DEREK** enters, holding a beer and talking into a microphone.)*

DEREK. Now I'm here with my friend, one of my BEST friends, and he doesn't want me to announce his name. He's shy. He doesn't want to come up here with me. But we all think he SHOULD, right?! He's a great singer! He's a PIANIST! Plus, he's got a big performance coming up in Two Days! We drove thirty miles away to come to THIS Karaoke Bar: it's the last stop on the wild train ride that is bro night. Can you give him a round of applause? Give him around of applause! *(Regardless of whether anyone does.)* WOOOOO!!!

> *(**BOBBIE** comes on stage, sheepishly, looking at the ground.)*

WOOOOOOOOO!!!! YEAAAAH!!!! LET'S DUET THIS BITCH!

> *(The karaoke music starts.)*

(DEREK and BOBBIE sing their favorite karaoke song in the style of "Mr. Jones" by Counting Crows[1].)

(The first verse: it's only DEREK singing.)

(BOBBIE mouths the occasional lyric, silently. Picks his middle fingernail.)

(Doesn't know what to do with his hands. Looks mostly at the ground, sometimes at the screen, occasional at DEREK. Never at the audience.)

(DEREK loves karaoke. He grooves to the music, not dancing, but grooving. He finds moments to hold the mic out to the audience. He bangs his head. He owns the stage. He might groove Around BOBBIE.)

(First chorus: still all DEREK.)

(Second verse: DEREK puts the mic in BOBBIE's hands.)

(BOBBIE won't sing. After a line or two of painful silence...)

DEREK. Come on, man!

(He pats BOBBIE on the back. BOBBIE sings, sheepishly. So nervous. Petrified.)

WOOOOOOOO!!!

---

1 A license to produce *Bobbie Clearly* does not include a performance license for "Mr. Jones" by Counting Crows. The publisher and author suggest that the licensee contact ASCAP or BMI to ascertain the music publisher and contact such music publisher to license or acquire permission for performance of the song. If a license or permission is unattainable for "Mr. Jones" the licensee may not use the song in *Bobbie Clearly* but may create an original composition in a similar style or use a similar song in the public domain. For further information, please see Music Use Note on page 3.

(Second Chorus: **BOBBIE** *checks in with* **DEREK**.*)*

(Smiles for the first time, nervously. He gains confidence.)

*(***DEREK*** *bites his bottom lip and grins.)*

(It's all **BOBBIE** *now.)*

(By the end of the second chorus, **BOBBIE** *is singing about half as loud as* **DEREK** *was, but still lacks* **DEREK***'s verve.)*

(Third Verse Or Final Chorus – basically until the end of the song: **BOBBIE** *gains confidence. He sings louder and louder. He has fun. He puts an arm around* **DEREK***, who gets a little freaked out by this and finds a moment, subtly, to not have* **BOBBIE***'s arm around him and stand separately.)*

*(***BOBBIE***'s having a great time!)*

(He's singing!)

(He's grooving!)

(He's loving the crowd!)

(The song ends.)

(Maybe there's applause. Maybe none.)

*(***BOBBIE*** *practically skips offstage.)*

DEREK. Thanks Everybody. Gooooooo Biiiiiiiiig Ree-eeeeed! GO! BIG! RED![1]

    *(***DEREK*** *exits.)*

    *(***DARLA*** *enters.)*

---

1. A Cornhusker cheer.

DARLA. Dear Bobbie,

Would you like to go to TGI Fridays with me? They have a lunch special on Sundays that gets you two meals and a sampler platter of appetizers plus two Cola's if you'd like it, all for Twenty-Five Dollars. My treat.

You haven't answered any of my telephone calls so I hope you don't mind me sliding this envelope under your front door.

Bobbie, I have a bad feeling about tomorrow. Please come have onion blossoms and hot wings with me at TGI Fridays.

Love,

Darla

End of Act Two

Intermission

ACT THREE

(Below the still suspended corn, a large banner hangs across the back of the stage:)

(WELCOME TO THE CASEY G. WELCH FOUNDATION'S 8TH ANNIVERSARY MEMORIAL TALENT SHOW!)

(A piano, a bench, and a microphone stand have been placed onstage too.)

(Clack.)

(Clack.)

(Clack.)

(Clack.)

(Clack.)

(Clack.)

(Clack.)

(EDDIE *walks out to the middle of the stage in tap shoes.)*

(Looks at us.)

(Pause.)

(Wait for it.)

EDDIE. One
 Two
 Three
 Four
 FIVE

SIX
SEVEN
EIGHT!

    (Music kicks in![1])

    *(***EDDIE*** *tap dances.)*

    (He's good.)

    (He has a smile.)

    (The music ends.)

    (Applause.)

    *(***EDDIE*** *approaches the microphone stand.)*

EDDIE. Thank you.

    (Takes a deep breath.)

I want to say something?
I heard about what happened to Bobbie last night.(?)
And that's pretty awful.
And I'm gonna take my time to grieve about it.
And even pray for him.(?) But Now Is Not That Time.
Today Is Supposed To Be About My Sister.
And <u>Us</u>.
This Community.
Milton.
Which we're All a part of whether we like it or not.
Thank you for honoring my sister.

    (Clack.)

    (Clack.)

    (Clack.)

---

1. A license to produce *Bobbie Clearly* does not include a performance
license for any third-party or copyrighted music. Licensees should create
an original composition or use music in the public domain. For further
information, please see Music Use Note on page 3.

(Clack.)

(Clack.)

(Clack.)

(Clack.)

(**EDDIE** *exits.*)

PETE. *(Enters smiling.)* WOW! That was great / Eddie!

MEGHAN. *(Enters smiling.)* Great job Eddie! I wish I could dance / like that!

PETE. For our next act we have two very strong AND proud members of our community! He's an AWESOME guitarist –

MEGHAN. And the other guy could probably help you out with your uh deer stand!

PETE. That's right, Meghan! *(They high five.)* Isn't she great? I think she's <u>so great!</u>

MEGHAN. *(Blushing?)* Aww, that's so sweet.

PETE. You're sweet. Well!

MEGHAN. Let's give it up for…

PETE & MEGHAN. RUSSSSS ANND STANNLEEEE EEEEYYYYY!!!

(**RUSS** *and* **STANLEY** *enter.*)

(**PETE** *and* **MEGHAN** *exit.*)

(**RUSS** *has a guitar.*)

RUSS. Hey ladies and gents!
Wow this talent show is, man.
So I don't have an act…
a SOLO ACT that is…
But Stanley and I are going to sing "Paradise By The Dashboard Light."
The acoustic –
J.K. Totally gotchu.

RUSS. Actually, *(Clears throat.)* this is the informative part of the afternoon, where we'd like to take a little time to tell you all about the uhm, the great things thee Casey G. Welch Foundation has been doing, in memory of Uhm.
Stanley, would you like to...?

> *(S)*
>
> *(I)*
>
> *(L)*
>
> *(E)*
>
> *(N)*
>
> *(C)*
>
> *(E)*

Okay, so we got uhm
if you look under your chairs there should be uhm
pamphlets that –

> *(Points to an audience member who's holding one.)*

She's *(or "He's")* got one.

> *(**RUSS** plays something on the guitar, accompanying himself.)*

We've taken these Talent Shows all over.
I remember Detroit specifically,
that Megabus ride and
Gah, we met this really amazing Tallahassee family and
Jane. Loved. Council Bluffs.
She's so great.
Yeah we raised ten thousand Bucks –
Dollars –
for that community and
Part of that goes to end – uhm get rid of guns.
Except.

Hunting's okay, of course.

And there's pledge amounts there,

If you all, uhm.(?)

So yeah. This

Gives you a little glimpse into what that money entrance fee is going toward.

To date, we've helped victims of uhm...

Stanley would you – ?

STANLEY. For this last part, take the hand of the person – Don't do that. Just look at the back of the head of the person in front of you and if you're in the front row imagine your favorite parent and I want you to pray for that person in front of you. Or whoever. Or if you don't believe in prayer then heck uhm, think about that human. I'm sure he or she or uhm is struggling with a lot so just.

Privately. Yeah.

We're all going through uhm.

Nobody's special.

So we should all pray for.

Every – *(one)*

RUSS. It's so unfortunate not everyone could be here today but we all have to keep in mind it's <u>possible</u> he put his own hand in the thresher.

> (**STANLEY** *looks at* **RUSS**.)

Thought I'd...say the elephant in the room that we're all...

We got an update from the uhm.

The hospital wasn't able to reattach anything.

They only found a few bits.

They didn't think it was a good idea for him to check out so early this morning, but hopefully he turns up soon.

Darla's out searching for him, I know, and we're all praying for...

    (...)

RUSS. WOO! RAISE THE ROOF! MILTON'S GOT TALENT!

    *(**RUSS** and **STANLEY** exit, separately.)*

    *(**MEGHAN** and **PETE** enter.)*

MEGHAN. That was beautiful, Russ. I'm praying for Bobbie, too.

Up next we have um everybody's favorite nurse.

PETE. *(Whispers.)* Is he here?

MEGHAN. *(Nods and whispers something inaudibly to **PETE** and points.)*

PETE. Awesome. Uhm. Yeah.

Let's give it up for Derek Nelson!

MEGHAN. Derek Nelson everybody.

    *(**DEREK** enters from the back, approaching the stage, carrying a unicycle.)*

    (He's been up all night.)

    (He hasn't slept.)

    (Is that blood on his shirt?)

    (When he gets to the stage...)

(Whispers.) Are you okay?

    *(**DEREK** whispers something inaudibly to **MEGHAN** and **PETE**.)*

PETE. *(Whispers.)* Yeah No. He's not here. I'm positive.

    *(**DEREK** whispers something inaudible.)*

MEGHAN. Bobbie's not here.

PETE. Derek are you sure you want to – ?

DEREK. It's okay. Yeah, it's – fine okay.(?) Right?

PETE. *(Whispers, nodding.)* yeah great.

    *(**PETE** and **MEGHAN** exit.)*

(**DEREK** *turns to face the audience.*)

DEREK. Did you know unicycling can be good for your core?

(…)

I got a voicemail from Bobbie at one in the morning.

(He gets out his cellphone and speakerphones it and plays the voicemail into the microphone.)

BOBBIE'S VOICEMAIL. "Sorry Derek you're probably asleep
I'm out at the cornfield
there's a lot of blood
hang on, I see you're calling."

(**DEREK** *ends it and pockets the phone.*)

DEREK. I listened to that in the gift shop at Methodists
Regional today.
I'm a little… *(Out of it.)*
I've been up all night
and this morning.

(He just stands there.)

(Seeing his town and himself in the town.)

I tell my daughter, "Just be nice to folks."(?)
Probably we all do, to our kids.(?)
Just be nice to the little girls in your class.
And those little bonehead boys.
And if somebody wrongs you girl
Daddy will do his best to fix it.
Nobody <u>wants</u> to hurt anybody.
<u>I</u> never –
<u>You</u> don't –
And that person, they're probably going through –
It can be hard.
So pray.
And try.
And.

DEREK. If everybody was just nice to everybody, everything would be good.
End quote.

> (**DEREK** *mic drops the unicycle.*)

> (*He exits.*)

> (*The unicycle is alone on stage for a beat.*)

> (…)

> (**MEGHAN** *and* **PETE** *enter.*)

MEGHAN. Ladies and Gentlemen, Up Next, reading from her – OUR brand new book that just dropped today on Amazon dot com. My B.F.F.

PETE & MEGHAN. MEGAAAAAN HANSOOOOOOON!

> (*Applause?* **PETE** *and* **MEGHAN** *exit with the unicycle.*)

> (**MEGAN** *comes onstage and sits on the bench next to the microphone stand.*)

> (*Clears throat.*)

MEGAN. Whatever Derek.

> (*She reads from* Pieces of Casey *in her whisper-book-reading voice, so serious, into the microphone.*)

"And in the wake of it all, in the wake of the <u>actual</u> wake, it finally began to feel real. I went with Meghan to her parents' house and we watched Mean Girls in their basement. And reflected."

> (*She turns a page.*)

"It was a warm night, balmy, and you could hear the crickets. We kept the windows open to stay cool, because Meghan's parents didn't have central air conditioning, and let the healing words of Tina Fey wash over us. My favorite scribe, I thought.
As we watched it – "

(This part isn't in the book, in her normal voice.) – and I don't know if any of you have seen Mean Girls but if you have, you know it's funny? but poignant.

(Back to the book and her book-reading voice.) "As we watched Mean Girls we realized: These characters? Were Us. I was Regina George, but nice. Meghan was one of the other two, a little bit of both, probably. And Casey, Casey was Lindsay Lohan. The little sparrow from Africa that we took under our wing, but who actually ended up teaching us a lot about ourselves, in the end."

> *(Clears throat.)*

"Sometimes, on balmy summer nights, or crisp winter late mornings, I think of that time. And I think of Casey."

> *(**BOBBIE** enters, unseen, behind **MEGAN**.)*

> *(All the fingers on his right hand are gone and the stump is wrapped in bandages and he still has a hospital wristband around his left wrist.)*

MITCH.*(A gasp from the back of the auditorium.)* Oh my god Megan...

MEGAN. Thank you. It was hard to write.

(From the book.) "I think, What would Casey be like today?

What would her hair be like?

> *(**PETE** hurries onstage behind **MEGAN**, unseen, and whispers something to **BOBBIE** and ushers him offstage.)*

Would she color it, or would it stay mousey brown?

What books would she read?

Would she like The Hunger Games?

Would she have a boyfriend?

Would she be <u>married</u> by now?

Or would she be an <u>Independent</u> Woman?

And sometimes I'll talk to Casey."

*(**BOBBIE** reenters, alone.)*

BOBBIE. *(Whispers.)* Megan.

(She sees him.)

It's supposed to be my turn on the roster. People thought I wasn't going to come I guess. I don't mind. Just letting you know that I'm – I'm going to start when you're done. You're doing a great job.

(He gives her one thumb up.)

*(Is **MEGAN** having a panic attack?)*

MEGAN. "And sometimes I'll talk to Casey.
I'll say, 'What's heaven like? Is it for real? Are there five people you meet there, like that book? Because I think you're going to be one of MY five people, Casey.' "
The end.

*(**MEGAN** exits.)*

BOBBIE. I would clap, but.

*(**BOBBIE** comes forward.)*

(He stands next to the piano.)

I'm really glad to be a part of today. When I had my accident yesterday, the first thing that popped into my mind was that maybe I wouldn't be able to perform. That was the worst thought. Cuz I've been so looking forward to this.

I was trying to decide, literally, actually all year what I would play on the piano, if I got to play. And I picked uhm, "The Scientist"? By Coldplay?

But that's okay now.

Well actually uhm. No.

It's okay.

I'm.

When I was getting better, there was this really fantastic Doctor, and we would do these therapy exercises. That I won't go into. Uhm. But. We would make these...and it was helpful because... You could pretend to...

Oh let me just show you.

(**BOBBIE** *walks offstage and reenters with a black duffel bag.*)

(*He unzips the bag.*)

(*Reaches in with his good hand.*)

(*Stops.*)

(*Takes his hand back out.*)

(*Looks at the audience.*)

I've always heard about these Talent Shows. And thought they were such a good idea.
And a good fundraiser.
But the sad part, I thought,
was that Casey could never be in one.
Because of me.
So, I thought, "What if Casey...

(*He fishes around in the duffel bag.*)

(*When his hand comes out it is inside a* **CASEY MUPPET.***)*

(*It is an amateurish yet lovingly crafted muppet, like something an overachieving twelve-year-old at a summer camp might make.*)

...Could be part of the Talent Show?"
Say "Hi" Casey.

(**BOBBIE** *speaks for* **CASEY** *in a girl voice.*)

CASEY. Hi Everybody.
BOBBIE. It's so good to see you! So, <u>IS</u> Heaven for real?
CASEY. It's Fuh Reel For Real, Bobbie.
BOBBIE. Cool. Uhm.
Casey, before anybody gets mad,
I want you to know that
I'm sorry.
I am so so sorry about everything.

> (**BOBBIE** *hugs* **CASEY**.)
>
> (*A pop can explodes against the piano next to* **BOBBIE**.)
>
> (**MITCH** *threw it.*)
>
> (*Quiet.*)

What would you like to do today?

CASEY. Well. I know that Mom's favorite performance of mine, oh my god so embarrassing, is when I was Gwendolen in The Importance of Being Earnest.

BOBBIE. You WERE so good in that.

CASEY. Really? Thank you.

I wasn't the lead but, you know, "there are no small parts."

BOBBIE. You STOLE the SHOW. I saw it five times. You're such a good actress and I – Hey, would you want to do a bit of The Importance of Being Earnest? Right now?

CASEY. But we don't have anybody from the original cast here.

BOBBIE. Well, I memorized the part of Jack. On my own time.

> (**STANLEY** *enters.*)
>
> (*This can take a long time.*)
>
> (**BOBBIE** *looks at him.*)
>
> (**STANLEY** *is so close to* **BOBBIE**.)
>
> (**STANLEY** *looks at the audience.*)
>
> (**BOBBIE** *waits.*)
>
> (**STANLEY** *exits.*)

CASEY. But Bobbie, you were supposed to help me use my arm.

BOBBIE. Oh that's right.

CASEY. I don't want to act without the full range of my powers, you know? I do a lot of arm acting. Maybe we could get somebody from the audience to come up and help.

BOBBIE. I don't know, Casey.

People don't like me very much.

CASEY. Bobbie, you have to start putting yourself out there. Remember, God has a bigger plan for you than you could <u>ever</u> imagine for yourself.

<u>End Quote.</u>

BOBBIE. Uhm, would anybody from the audience like to come up?

>*(The rest of* **BOBBIE***'s line can take a long time.)*

To help Casey?

Pete?

Mitch?

I see you in the back there.

Megan?

Meghan with an H?

Derek?

Okay.

Well –

A MAN'S VOICE OFFSTAGE. I'll Help.

>*(Clack.)*

>*(Clack.)*

>*(Clack.)*

>*(Clack.)*

>*(Clack.)*

>*(Clack.)*

>*(Clack.)*

>**(EDDIE** *enters from the wings in tap shoes.)*

EDDIE. I'll help you, Bobbie.

> *(Silence.)*

> (**BOBBIE** *is a little stunned by this.*)

BOBBIE. Thank you.

EDDIE. No problem. Happy to help.
I think this is what everybody was hoping for, right?
Great job, Pete.
You're one of us now, Bobbie.
Welcome back.

BOBBIE. Can we have a round of applause for Eddie?

> *(Quiet?)*

EDDIE. Okay so I just grab this little stick here?

CASEY. Yeah, it's attached to my hand.

EDDIE. And move it around?

CASEY. Yeah when I'm talking. When I'm saying my lines
for expressive purposes. Like that. There. You're getting
the hang of it. "To beeee, or NOT to beeeee!" Great job,
Bro.

EDDIE. Thanks Casey.

CASEY. *(To* **EDDIE**.*)* I've missed you, Eddie. You've grown up
so much.
I'm proud of you.

BOBBIE. Casey, do you think we can maybe all be friends?

CASEY. Best friends.
Should we start Bobbie?

BOBBIE I think I'm ready.

CASEY. Don't be nervous, Eddie.
Just picture everybody in the audience completely
naked.

> *(Then, in a British accent...)*

BOBBIE AS JACK. Charming day it has been, Miss Fairfax.

CASEY AS GWENDOLEN. Pray don't talk to me about the
weather, Mr. Worthing. Whenever people talk to me
about the weather,

MITCH IN THE AUDIENCE.

BOOOOOOOOOOO!

BOOOOOOOOOOO!

BOOOOOOOOOOO!

Get Off The STAGE!!!

EDDIE ARE YOU
JUST GOING TO – ?!

CASEY AS GWENDOLEN.

I always feel quite uhm uh uh uh certain that they mean something else

And That Makes Me So Nervous.

BOBBIE AS JACK.

I do mean something else.

CASEY AS GWENDOLEN.

I thought so. In fact, I am never –

(**EDDIE** *raises his hand, stiff arm, palm out, silencing* **MITCH.**)

(Q)

(U)

(I)

(E)

(T)

(Waits to make sure.)

(Lowers his hand and takes the stick again.)

EDDIE. Continue.

BOBBIE. Would you like to hold her?

(**BOBBIE** *puts* **CASEY** *in* **EDDIE**'s *arms.*)

BOBBIE AS JACK. Miss Fairfax, ever since I met you I have admired you more than any girl...
I have ever met since... I met you.

CASEY AS GWENDOLEN. We live, as I hope you know, Mr. Worthing, in an age of ideals –

EDDIE. Stop.
    I have a question.
BOBBIE. Can It Wait?
EDDIE. *(An outburst.)* NO!
BOBBIE. We're in the middle of our –
EDDIE. I've helped you.
    Let me ask my one question.

        (Silence.)

MITCH IN THE AUDIENCE. <u>ASK HIM.</u>
EDDIE. *(Whispers something inaudible.)*

        (Quiet.)

        *(**BOBBIE** says nothing.)*

        (Whispers the same thing inaudibly.)

MITCH IN THE AUDIENCE. <u>WE CAN'T HEAR YOU.</u>
EDDIE. Why?
CASEY AS GWENDOLEN. And MY ideal has always been to
    LOVE someone of the name of –
EDDIE. *(Screams.)*

        (Tries to restrain himself.)

        (Pounds on the floor.)

        (Screams again.)

        *(Beats **BOBBIE** with the muppet.)*

Guess what number I'm thinking of?!
GUESS! GUESS!
You monster! You piece of shit!
Are you happy Pete?!
Are you people happy?!

        (Hurls the muppet.)

        *(Slaps **BOBBIE** across the face repeatedly.)*

        (Sobs.)

*(Beats **BOBBIE** with fists.)*

BOBBIE. HELP! HELP! HELP! HELP! / HELP! HELP!

PETE. *(Who has run onstage.)* Hey! Hey! / Hey! Hey

BOBBIE. / *(Screaming.)*

PETE. *(Pulling **EDDIE** off of **BOBBIE**.)* EddieEddie/Eddie –

MITCH. *(Entering.)* HEY!

*(**MITCH** tackles **PETE**.)*

BOBBIE. SOMEBODY!

EDDIE. You come into our town / on her*

BOBBIE. Stop!

EDDIE. *day?! Huh?! We have a right / to know!*

BOBBIE. *(Cries.)*

PETE. Eddie, STOP / IT!

EDDIE. *You want to be a part of this!(?)

BOBBIE. I don't want / AHH! AAAHHHHH

EDDIE. *(On top of **BOBBIE**, bashing his face in.)* her her her her / her her her*

PETE. Mitch! Get off of me!

EDDIE. *her / her her*

MEGAN IN THE AUDIENCE. We don't feel sorry for you!

EDDIE. *her her / her her her her her her her her her

BOBBIE. Derek! Derek! DEREK! DEREK!

DEREK. *(Running onstage and pulling **EDDIE** off of **BOBBIE**.)* YOU KNOW WHAT MAN I THINK MAYBE WE SHOULD ALL JUST WRAP THIS / UP!

MITCH. *(Standing.)* I want to know!

PETE. *(Standing, bloody nose.)* You're being a fucking asshole!

You fucking psychopath!

Bobbie, it's / okay.

MITCH. Are you people insane?!*

BOBBIE. *(Sobs.)*

MITCH. *Are you people listening to / yourself?!

PETE. *(To* BOBBIE.*)* I'm really glad that you're here!

DEREK. Me too! I wanna know what happens to Gwen/
dolen!

MEGHAN. *(Entering.)* Hey guys! Uhm! This has been
SUCH a Memorable Talent Show but, hey, we should –

> (DARLA *enters in uniform.)*

DARLA. <u>I Think It's Time For Everybody To Leave.</u>
<u>Everybody.</u>
Starting with you, Bobbie.

> (BOBBIE *exits.)*

Derek, go with him.

DEREK. Me?

DARLA. I said Go.

> (DEREK *exits.)*

> (RUSS *exits.)*

> (MEGAN *exits.)*

> (MEGHAN *exits.)*

> (PETE *exits.)*

> (MITCH *exits.)*

> (EDDIE *exits.)*

> (DARLA *is alone.)*

"That's all folks,"
was the last thing I said.
And then the curtain fell.

An

acre

of

corn

falls

like

a

curtain

from

the

sky.

DARLA. That was
>   One
>   Two
>   Three
>   years ago.
>   Wow.
>   So I'm your last interview, huh?
>   Some honor.
>   Get in the squad car.
>   I'll take you to see the Town Nativity.

>   *(It's nighttime.)*

>   Look.
>   Everybody's Christmas Lights are finally up.
>   They're even prettier this year than last.
>   Here's Main Street.
>   There's the Post Office.
>   That's where the old water tower used to be.
>   It was blue.
>   This is the house where I grew up.
>   …
>   Last time I saw Bobbie it was about a month after the
>   Talent Show.
>   So three years ago.
>   Thereabouts.
>   I picked him up at his cousin's and took him to get TGI
>   Fridays.
>   We got a booth.
>   And ate so much food.
>   Onion blossoms and hot wings.
>   Mozzarella sticks.
>   Shrimp.
>   Fries.
>   Quesadillas.
>   Loaded potato skins.

Ahi Tuna Crisps.
Siracha Chicken Potstickers.
Tuscan Spinach Dip.
Did I say quesadillas?
All finger food because he wasn't left-handed.
Bobbie was so happy for that hour and a half.
He said, "I wish we could live here."
They'd fired him from the flytrap factory.
And he'd stopped going to church.
The parish asked him not to come anymore.
He told me he stood outside once, secretly,
but it hurt too much to hear the piano.
That had always been the one thing – His talent.
This is the practice football field.
And here's the Nativity.
You mind if we park here?

> *(Members of the town enter and take their
> places.)*

> *(Some, like* **DEREK**, **MEGHAN**, *and* **MEGAN**
> *are dressed as characters from the Nativity.
> Others are spectators and wear normal winter
> clothes. It should not be literal. The tableau
> should give an equal sense of the participants
> and the spectators. Everyone is still.* **JANE** *and*
> **EDDIE** *are not there.)*

> **(THE NATIVITY** *sings "There's A Wideness In
> God's Mercy.")*

Look at Derek. He's so blitzed.
Doesn't Meghan look perfect as Mary?
There's Mr. Welch, parked in his Chevy.
I wonder who's that with the Florida plates.(?)
After TGI Fridays I drove Bobbie back to his cousin's
house.

DARLA. One of the windows had been smashed in for a week
and somebody had shot all of his dogs.
The cousin had given Bobbie a month to clear out.
He said before Christmas.
Bobbie asked to live with Derek but Derek said that
was a bridge too far.
Which I understand.
He asked me, "Can I see your house, Darla, and keep
hanging out?"
So I took him. We sat in my living room with that ugly
olive 70s carpet I've never replaced.
I showed him the musical saw that George used to play.
He was a real musician, my George.
And Bobbie marveled at his old piano in the sun room,
which I hadn't touched in years.
He traced a B in the dust on the top.
He asked to see an old photo album, so I showed him
our wedding pictures.
Now I wasn't in uniform for any of this.
Civilian clothes, you know. Off duty.
And he asked, "Where do you keep your uniform?"
I said, "In the closet upstairs."
And he asked, "Where do you keep your gun?"
And I looked at him, sitting in George's chair across the
room.
And he looked at me.
And I knew what he wanted.
And I thought about it.
For a long time.

        (**DARLA** *listens to the hymn.*)

        (*It sounds far away.*)

        (*She doesn't speak for a while.*)

Finally I said, "Bobbie, it's time for you to go."
I drove him back to his cousin's house.

And started making arrangements.
So now he's up north at that facility for people who
can't deal with real life.
I still write him once a month but I never have visited.
I might though, next month, maybe, before I move.
I'm retiring in January.
Nobody knows this yet.
I'm going to stay with my brother in Kansas.
I'd like to be closer to family.
I will miss it, though.
There's not a lot of places like Milton.
All my life is here.
I hope I've been a good cop.
Life is impossible for some people.
I mean life has become...
It's impossible.
And why is that?

    (The hymn ends.)

    (Quiet.)

End of Play